For

JAMES EUAN

J.

CATALOGUE NO. 3990/U

PRINTED BY JAS. TRUSCOTT & SON LTD., LONDON AND TONBRIDGE

WAU-WAU
THE APE

BY

JOAN KIDDELL-MONROE

METHUEN & CO. LTD., LONDON
36 Essex Street, Strand, W.C.2

1947

PRINTED IN GREAT BRITAIN

WAU-WAU
THE APE

BY

JOAN KIDDELL-MONROE

METHUEN & CO. LTD., LONDON
36 Essex Street, Strand, W.C.2

1947

PRINTED IN GREAT BRITAIN

" He flies through the air with the greatest of ease."

Away in the Far East at the tail-end of Java lies the small volcanic isle of Bali.   It is a fantastic little island, brilliant with tropical sunshine and vivid colour.   In its dense rain-forests tangled with trailing vines, grow plants that look like birds, and flowers like snakes, and queer pale fungi.

Here live the Gibbons, the Apes whom the ancient Greeks called Hylobates, " the Walkers in the Woods."

Wau-Wau the Ape, a tiny puce-grey gibbon with a black face, clung, as all baby gibbons do, to his mother's breast as she hurried through the tree-tops. His mother went very fast, barely touching the branches as she swung from tree to tree. She was so swift she could have caught the birds on the wing.

With his little hands twined in his mother's long hair, Wau-Wau sailed safely along. When he looked down he saw the steamy tangled jungle lying far, far below, so he hugged his mother tightly, and looking up watched the changing pattern of leaves against the sky.

Wau-Wau's mother could travel through the forest like this for hours without tiring, but swinging along-along-along made the little ape drowsy, and when a great butterfly that might have been cut out of rich black velvet came fluttering slowly by, Wau-Wau yawned, and sleepily stretching his hands to catch it . . . . forgot to hold on to his mother.

Down he dropped.

"Mamma, Mamma," he shrieked, but his
mother could not stop in mid-air to save him.

Down, down, down, down through the swaying branches and the rustling leaves, and a shower
of blossoms floated silently after him. Faster and
faster, the further he fell the faster he went, and the
jungle drew nearer and nearer. Now Wau-Wau
was too frightened to shriek any more; he clutched
at every vine and twig, but they tore from his grasp
and he still went on falling, till at last he managed
to catch hold of a branch and grip it tight. The
branch began wriggling under his
fingers, and a voice hiss-ss-sed
indignantly,
"Let go of my tail."

Wau-Wau let go as
quick as he could,

and the slender silver tree-snake went to sleep
again . . . .

       but the poor little ape sprawled
on a bough of the tree way down below, with all
the breath knocked out of his thin little puce-grey
body.

Miserably the tiny gibbon wondered how did his mother sail so easily through the tree-tops? Perhaps if he tried very hard he could do the same, and after a while, when he grew tired of sitting on his particular branch, he made a timid leap for another. And another. And almost before he had time to think, he was swinging along from bough to bough like gibbons always do.

Gaily Wau-Wau swung through the forest. Sometimes he slid down a vine to pick a nice ripe banana, or gather some nuts, but he always sped back into the branches again very, very quickly. Then Wau-Wau spied a strange thing hanging in a teak tree, and being always inquisitive, swarmed up to look at it.

II

The thing had been woven of twigs and grasses with an opening left at the top, and we should have said looked just like an old sock. Wau-Wau wondered what it could be, for he'd not seen anything like it before. He approached very cautiously and peered all around it. It didn't move, so he squinted into the opening, but couldn't see what might be inside. Then he put in his hand and his fingers touched something smooth and warm. He pulled it out; it was an egg.

The little ape turned the egg over and over, admiring the colour; then he cracked the shell and gobbled it up.

Wau-Wau was feeling to see if there were any more eggs when the Weaver Birds returned. Screaming with rage, the two birds flew at the little ape who was robbing their nest, and they tried to peck him and beat him with their wings.

Wau-Wau was scared, and scrambled quickly away, not knowing the Weaver Birds were frightened too, for gibbons like to eat plump little birds as well as their eggs, and he didn't stop till he reached the ground.

Close on the ground it was hot and steamy.
Broad leaves shut out the sun, making a green
gloom full of shadows.

Wau-Wau felt very small and alone. His
mother had always carried him when they came
down out of the trees to drink at the little stream
that struggled through the forest. Now he found
when he stood up his arms were too *long*. They
reached to his toes, and got in the way when he
tried to walk.

The little gibbon wrinkled his ugly little black
face in dismay.

Rustling, whispering noises came from the grasses and bushes, but as nobody appeared Wau-Wau grew bolder. Holding his arms awkwardly in the air, he set out to explore.

A grotesque little figure Wau-Wau made as he ran along with his long, long arms waving above his head.

He peeped into pitcher plants,
and sniffed at orchids,

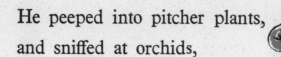

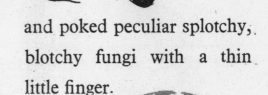

and poked peculiar splotchy,
blotchy fungi with a thin
little finger.

And he nibbled at leaves like
thick pink flannel. Broad
spotty leaves and narrow
stripey leaves, and leaves
that looked like red patent
leather, for nearly everything looks like something
else in the rain-forests on
Bali, but he didn't care for any of them.

Then Wau-Wau found how easy
it was to keep his arms out of the way
if he crossed his hands at the back of
his neck, and this is the way gibbons
mostly walk when they are on the
ground, for gibbons are the only apes
who always walk erect like human
beings.

So the little gibbon ran on, poking
his nose or long thin fingers into
everything, and finding a neat
smooth coil lying in his path he
poked that too,
and was frightened again when Cobra
raised his wicked head and spread out
his hood.

Gradually the forest became dim and eerie. Leaves shone like tarnished metal and hung heavy as lead.

Wau-Wau felt uneasy and ran here and there whimpering for his mother. Darker and darker it grew, and a muttering and rumbling crept through the trees. Suddenly a flash lit the forest with vivid white light, and Wau-Wau saw a gecko standing as though petrified, on a stone.

Then a tremendous clap of thunder shook the forest from end to end. The flowers trembled and all the leaves jangled.

The little ape dived under a bush. Cowering amongst the twisted roots, Wau-Wau watched. When the next flash came he saw a big hairy-legged spider creeping up a vine. It was a

bird-eating spider, creeping up to catch a tiny honey-bird sheltering in the bush. With each flash the little ape saw the spider creeping closer. He wondered if he should catch it and have it for his dinner ; but it was such a big spider, and so very, very hairy, he thought he wouldn't.

Whilst Wau-Wau was thinking this the thunder rumbled away into the distance and the forest grew light again. The honey-bird twittered and flew away, and a lonely little kantjil ran crazily through the woods.

Wau-Wau crawled out of his hiding place and climbed up into the sunlit branches. He had already forgotten the storm ; animals don't remember things for very long, and gibbering happily to himself he went swinging on his way and soon reached the edge of the forest.

Looking out through the leaves he saw a little plain bordered with flowering shrubs. Tall alang-alang grass turned the plain into a lake of swaying silver, and clusters of trees made dark islands. Beyond the plain, mountains drew a jagged line against the sky, and Wau-Wau saw a thin wisp of smoke curling lazily into the still air from the highest peak, and a small cloud hovering like a shadowy wreath around it.

It was a volcano.

Quite suddenly the sun slid out of the sky,
and it was night on the little island of Bali.

When all the gibbons gathered for their
evening song, one sang alone. A weird,
pathetic song. It was Wau-Wau's mother
mourning her lost baby.

By this time Wau-Wau was a very tired little ape. He heard the harsh voices of the gibbons far away in the forest, but he didn't know where or how to find them. So he huddled forlornly in his tree and fell asleep.

23

He awoke in the night and heard a Tiger padding softly round the foot of the tree.

Somewhere in the moonlight Wild-Cat yowled. Wau-Wau shivered, and a bunch of flying-foxes hanging from the branch beside him roused themselves yawning, and unfolding their cloaks flitted silently away into the darkness.

Across the plain the thin wisp had grown to a
thick billowing volume of black smoke, and the
small cloud glowed a fiery red.

The little ape's eyes were heavy, he couldn't
keep awake, so he didn't hear the volcano grum-
bling, or see the showers of sparks it
tossed into the sky.

The sun was up when Wau-Wau woke again, and he started to shout and sing, though it was late in the morning for a gibbon to be singing. But his voice was so small it got lost amongst the screeching of a family of grass-green parrots in the next tree, and the chirping of hundreds of birds who were waking up all around.

He breakfasted on leaves and fruit, and took a long drink from the stream where it cascaded over some stones into a shallow pool, with thick ferns and curious flowers growing on its spongy, mossy banks. Then capered back to the edge of the forest.

Squeezing through the
flowery border, Wau-Wau
found the silvery alang-alang
grass was taller than he. He hesitated timidly,
but a handsome hare came bouncing along and
with a flick of his ears disappeared amongst the
grass; so the little gibbon ambled after him into
the queer, pale world between the stalks.

The hare had quite vanished, and soon Wau-
Wau was lost, for all ways looked alike. There
was nothing but the stalks and the whispering of
the grass above his head.

A big brown rat came scurrying by, paused for
an instant to regard him
with bright, boot-button
eyes, and scampered on.
And a tiny shrew-mouse,
her nose twitch-twitching
all the time, darted from
under a weed and was
gone in a flash.

Then Wau-Wau got scared all alone with the rustling, whispering grass, and he started to run. In a panic he ran, and tripped and fell, and ran on again till he came to a clump of tall lontar palms, and he swarmed up one of these useful trees as quickly as he could.

Now the natives of Bali value this palm enormously, for from it they get timber, and sago, and sugar, and they dry its broad leaves and use them for writing on. But Wau-Wau didn't mind if they were useful or not; feeling safe once more he played a little game all by himself, swooping from tree to tree,

and back again,

and when he tired of
this he curled up and
went to sleep.

The little puce-grey gibbon woke
up feeling very hungry, so he leapt down
out of the palm tree and ran quickly
through the last little bit of alang-alang
grass into the open country. Now everything was different again. Wau-Wau forgot his
hunger and ran along with short, skippy steps, or,
if there were trees, climbed into the branches and
swung along, until he came to a plantation of
sugar cane. He broke a piece from one of the canes
and nibbled it as he went. On all sides were
fields of coffee, sugar canes and tobacco, and the
green-terraced hillsides looked like hanging gardens.

A family of wild pigs scampered past looking
for juicy crops to plunder, and Wau-Wau hid in a
tree till they had gone by.

Once Wau-Wau saw a huge water
buffalo who seemed to be asleep, standing knee-deep in a stream. And he
found fantastic little carved and gilded
temples, but he couldn't see in, because Balinese
temples always have two doorways, and the inside
one is never in line with the one outside,
so that evil spirits cannot enter,
for, as everyone knows,
evil spirits can only
travel in a straight
line.

And when it was night again
he came to a village and heard
music.

The inquisitive little ape climbed into a tree and looked down on the strangest sight.

A blazing fire lit up the centre of the village, and in the flickering light men were leaping in a weird dance. And each man had a long tail sticking out behind him.

They were dancing the Monkey Dance.

In the shadow of the huts the villagers sat watching, and musicians played curious bamboo instruments and drums.

Unnoticed by anyone, Wau-Wau slipped down and joined the dancers. He followed behind imitating their gestures, and though he almost *was* really a monkey, he was the only one without a tail.

All at once a demon king appeared. He was hideous and terrible. The little ape was terrified by the dreadful apparition ; how was he to know that the demon king, like the monkey men, was only a make-believe character in a play, for the Balinese people, believing in good and evil spirits, and witches, and all kinds of magic, perform these plays whenever it is a Holy Day. And they have an enormous number of Holy Days.

So Wau-Wau gave a piercing yell and leapt into the shadows. Three little dancing-girls who were sitting entranced waiting for it to be their turn to dance, screamed as he flashed past. They thought he was a flying-cat, and like all natives, feared the flying-cat, thinking it had power to fascinate them.

Away in the tree-tops fled the little gibbon.
The hub-bub in the village faded into silence behind
him and, because he was scared, Wau-Wau wanted
his mother.

Every now and then he stopped to call
" MAMMA " in a shrill little frightened voice.
Nobody answered, and he flitted on like a small
grey ghost through the night.

" MAMMA . . . . MAMMA . . . . "

In the morning Wau-Wau stood on the sea-shore and saw the wide Indian Ocean sparkling in the sun. Tall mangroves fringed the shore, and dwarf nipa palms, those trees whose wood is, so surprisingly, so much lighter than cork, tossed their feathery heads in the soft breeze from the sea.

The little ape ran eagerly down to the water's edge and took a long drink. But the water tasted salty. He didn't like it and spat it out again.

The fish who lived amongst the coral
down in the deep blue sea saw his
little wobly reflection
wavering above
them

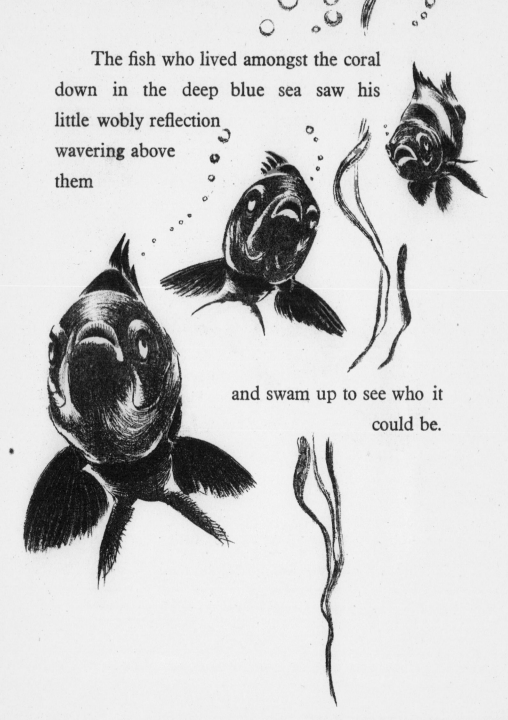

and swam up to see who it
could be.

But Wau-Wau didn't linger. He hurried along the beach calling, calling all the time.

A party of pelicans fishing in one of the shallow pools left behind by the sea gaped at him in surprise, and all the little fish they'd caught in their bills wriggled out and fell back into the pool.

On and on wandered the little lost ape, and perhaps there *are* good spirits after all, and one of them guided him back past thatched villages on stilts, where people in brightly patterned sarongs were gayer than flowers,

and past dozens of little gilded temples and wayside shrines, to his own forest.

The grass-green parrots were circling in
great clouds, still shrilly screeching.

Wau-Wau swung wearily into a tree. A sad-faced gibbon sat disconsolately on one of the branches, peering at every little ape who passed.

" MAMMA," shrieked Wau-Wau, flinging himself into her arms,

and they went swinging away

through the tree-tops.